Johnny Nichols...
I want to play baseball

Written by

Marie A. Cavallaro

Illustrated by

John Cleary

ISBN# 978-0-9905817-1-0
All illustrations by permission of the artist John Cleary
This is an expanded and revised edition of the original book published in 2008, ISBN 978-0-9905817-0-3
Printed In PRC

Dedicated to...

My Son,
Ian Nicholas Quillen

Little Johnny Nichols woke up on a bright, sunshiny spring day. Usually, he waited for the sound of his mom's voice calling him to breakfast, but not this morning. This was the day of tryouts for the Newtown "Cubs" baseball team.

Johnny leaped out of bed, scrambled through his closet to find his favorite baseball shirt, pants, shoes and socks. He dressed himself in a flash...

...and tore through the house and out of the kitchen door with his dog, Rusty, at his heels.

Mom had just enough time to get out of the way, so she would not be trampled by all those feet and paws charging through the kitchen.

The little league baseball field was only two blocks away.

When they arrived, the other boys were waiting at the gate to try out for the team. Johnny stood in line with the others.

When he reached the coach's table to sign up, the coach raised his head and said, "I'm sorry son, you are not big enough for the team - maybe next year."

Johnny was disappointed. He hung his head, dragged his feet and walked slowly away from the coach's desk.

The other fellows tried to make Johnny feel better. They told him to come to all the practices and games, so that next year he would be sure to make the team.

Ted, a pitcher, said, "Here kid, take my cap." Another player, Mike, thought that Johnny should have a team tee shirt

with his own number. "Let's give him the number 1." The number suited Johnny because he was so small.

Johnny thanked the fellows for the gifts, but he was still sad that he didn't make the team.

Johnny went, day after day, to watch the Cubs practice. From behind the fence he practiced, too. He pretended he was up at bat, firmly planting his feet in the ground while grasping the bat as the other players did.

He waited patiently for just the right pitch and swung at it, making a "pop" sound. He imagined the ball soaring through the sky, back, back, back, and out of the stadium for a home run. He listened for the cheers from the imaginary crowd as he rounded the pretend bases.

Sometimes Johnny even pretended to be the pitcher. He waited for the signal from the catcher, wound up raising his arms way over his head and pitched the ball with all of his might over home plate squarely

in the catcher's mitt. "Strike three, you're out!" he could almost hear the umpire shout. He imagined striking out three batters in a row!

At home, Johnny often practiced with his mom and dad, and even with his dog, Rusty. Mom played the pitcher while Dad was the batter. Johnny played the outfield, and Rusty guarded first base.

Finally, the day of the first game arrived. The Cubs were playing the Bulldogs from the next town. The stadium filled with fans of both teams and, even though Johnny wasn't on the team, he wore the team hat and shirt that his friends on the team had given him.

Johnny wanted so much to be in that game. He stood right up to the fence and watched each inning with excitement. He cheered for his friends, giving them lots of support.

Johnny could hardly believe how quickly the game was passing. Before he knew it, it was the last inning.

The Cubs were winning one to nothing. The Bulldogs had one more chance. There were two outs and two men on base, and their very best hitter came up to bat.

The coach of the Cubs called for a time out. The outfielder had twisted his ankle and had to leave the game.

Johnny was too excited to stand still. He decided to take a short run to help him calm down before the game began again.

Johnny and Rusty skirted around the back side of the field and came across a hole that was dug under the outfield wall. Rusty ran right for the hole and made it bigger. It was suddenly big enough for a small person, and Johnny was just the right size.

He wiggled under the wall and through the hole only to find himself in the outfield of the baseball stadium! With a new man in the outfield, the umpire signaled for the game to continue. It was a dream come true for, by accident, Johnny replaced the injured ball player and was now in the game!!!

The pitcher wound up, threw the ball and "pop" the batter sent the ball higher and higher, right toward Johnny in the outfield.

Keeping his eye on the ball, Johnny moved back, back, back until he backed into the outfield wall. It looked as if the ball was gone.

But then, at just the right moment, Johnny jumped as high as he could into the air and stretched his arm as far as it could go. Plunk!!! He did it! He caught the ball! He won the game!

Johnny heard the crowd roar with delight. The other team members all ran toward their hero and, as they got closer to Johnny, they were shocked to see the number 1 on his uniform. "It's Johnny!!!" they shouted.

Ted picked up Johnny, put him on his shoulders and paraded him across the field. The other players cheered Johnny and all agreed that he surely earned a place on the team.

The coach came over to Johnny and shook his hand. "You might be small," he said, "but you sure can play baseball!"

Then, as he turned to go back to the dugout, he stopped and said to Johnny, "Oh, by the way, welcome to the team!"

From the Author:

At the age of 2 my son was involved with baseball. I ironed many numbers onto every set of baseball pajamas. Every day he would go off to nursery school suited up to play baseball. Of course, no other child his age had the same passion.

Finding books about baseball was a real challenge. The biography of Hank Aaron was read over and over for a year and a half. Finally, this children's book was born. *Johnny Nichols* not only touches on a love for playing baseball but encourages good sportsmanship, persistence, family support and mere luck.

After 20 years on the bench, my son, who is now a college graduate, launched into his career as a sports journalist. For him, I give this book. Never give up on your passions and dreams...play ball!

Marie Cavallaro, Professor Emerita of Art at Salisbury University, is also the author of *Johnny Nichols: Special Gifts, Special Friends.* Contact at ccart1@live.com for more information.

Illustrator - John Cleary

Play ball! Finally!

Editor - Nicholas A. Cavallaro

Johnny Nichols teaches us the basic principals of a successful life. Never give up...recognize and seize the opportunities when they appear.

Graphic Artist - Beth Hébert

What a fantastic journey this has been! May all readers gather as much inner strength and passion for life as Johnny Nichols.

Thanks to...

Susan Cabral
Nicolas A. Cavallaro
John Cleary
Josh Davis
Beth Hébert
Iris Powell
Ian Quillen
Tom & Tara Ruch
Donelle Sawyer

The End

In Memory of
Nicholas J. Cavallaro
Athlete, Patriot, Father